Selected
Fairy Tales

Compiled by

'KUNWAR' ANIL KUMAR

MANOJ PUBLICATIONS

CONTENTS

Manoj Publications

761, Main Road Burari, Delhi-110084
Phone : 27611116, 27611349
Fax : 27611546, Mobile : 9868112194
E-mail : manojpublications@vsnl.net
Website : www.manojpublications.com

ISBN : 81-8133-409-4

Showroom :

1583-84, Dariba Kalan,
Chandani Chowk, Delhi-6
Phone : 23262174, 23268216
Mobile : 9818753569

Printers :
Jain Offset Printers

KIND LITTLE GIRL

ONCE there was a little girl in a village who was very generous and kind-hearted. She was an orphan but the whole world seemed to belong to her. She loved everyone and was loved by everyone.

But the sad part of her life was that she had no house to live in. One day she felt so discontented that she left her village without telling anyone. She set out into a forest with only a piece of bread in her hand.

The little girl had walked only a little distance when she saw an old man sitting by the side of the road. The old man was physically infirm and looked like a living structure of bones only. He was not capable of earning his bread and butter. He was begging.

"O dear little sweet girl! I am an old man. There is no one to take care of me. I am not capable of earning my bread and butter. I haven't had anything to eat for the last three days. I am starving. Please have mercy on me and give me something to eat," said the old man.

Though the little girl herself was very hungry and had kept the piece of bread so that she could assuage her hunger when she felt terribly hungry, she gave it to the old man.

"Sir, I wish I could give you more but this is all I had. Kindly accept whatever little I have," said the little girl and walked on without even waiting to be thanked.

Hardly had she walked a little distance when she happened to see a small boy shivering with cold.

Kind-hearted and generous as she was, she went to the small boy and said, "You seem to be shivering with cold. Tell me if there is anything that I could do for you."

"Yes, sister! It's extremely cold out here. I have no place where I could take shelter. I shall be only too grateful to you if you could kindly give me something to cover my head with," said the small boy.

The little girl smiled and gave her hat to the small boy. This provided him great relief.

"I wish everyone had a sister like you; you are so kind and generous," said the boy expressing his gratitude. "May God bless you."

The little girl didn't say anything. She simply gave a sweet and hypnotic smile and walked on.

As if the little girl was being put to test by divine, she met yet another shivering child in the woods. This time it was a small girl who had only a vest on her body.

Seeing her in so pitiable a condition, the little girl gave her skirt, fondled her with affection and said, "Don't worry my little sister! God will take care of you."

Now the little girl had only a vest left on her body. She herself started shivering with cold. But she was happy that she had been able to help so many in a day. She continued walking without any destination in her imagination.

It was getting dark now. The moon was also in a mood of playing hide and seek behind clouds. It was becoming difficult to see things around. But there didn't seem to be anything that could check her from moving ahead; ahead towards an unknown destination. Suddenly she heard someone sobbing.

"Who could it be?" she muttered to herself. She stopped and looked around. "Oh, there you are, little child!" The little girl had located a small child standing absolutely naked behind a big tree.

"What makes you weep, little brother? Oh, I see! You have no clothes on. O God! Have mercy on this child. How can you allow so small a child to have no clothes on to ward off the cold of such wintry night?" said the little girl in a choked voice.

"Sister! It's terribly cold," said the child weeping and sobbing, "Have pity on me. Kindly help me."

"Yes, dear child! I shall give you my vest, which is the only thing I have on me left; but I know you need it more than I do," saying this the little girl gave away her vest also, and now she had not even a thread on her body.

But she didn't stop; she kept on moving. And walking thus, she reached into a clearing of the forest, from where she could see the open sky, the moon playing hide and seek with clouds, and the stars twinkling.

By now it had become unbearably cold. She had begun shivering uncontrollably. She lifted pious eyes to heaven, sighed deeply and said with tears rolling down her cheeks—

"O Almighty God! I don't really know what instincts have guided me to this place. But I somehow have a very strong feeling that if I talk to you from here, I shall be listened to. The snow-clad mountains around me, the beautiful oak trees pointing towards the sky, the quiet lake before me, the moon and the stars, are all a witness to my prayers offered to you," saying this she began sobbing. It took her a little time to become normal. She said again—"God! can you tell me why you took away my parents when I needed them most? What fun was it making me an orphan? The whole of the universe belongs to you and you could not give me even a small house to live in. And not only that; you even took away the only piece of bread I had in my hand; you have so many small children without clothes in this wintry night that I had no alternative but to give away all my clothes one by one to those hapless children, and the result is that I am standing absolutely naked before you."

The little girl paused for a moment and then said in a choked voice, "I have never complained to you, but it doesn't mean that I have no feelings; I don't miss my parents; but..."

She would have continued thus had there been no interruption from the above—

"My sweet little child! I am aware of your plights," the voice was coming from the heavens.

The little girl looked up; the voice continued...

"...but you are my creation. You have been specially sent to earth. And such children of mine, who are sent to earth with a special purpose, are subjected to most severe tests. I am proud of you my child! You have passed all your tests successfully. Now you are dressed in very beautiful clothes. Just look at yourself."

The little girl looked at herself and was surprised to see herself dressed in the most exquisite manner. Now it was God's turn. He was showing miracles after miracles. There were most dainty dishes laid before her. Again there was a voice, a divine communication—"My child! I am sending your parents to join in supper. They will be with you for one whole night. And also...I promise to allow your parents to visit you once in a month when you come here, and they will stay with you throughout the night."

And lo, indeed her parents were standing before her. They hugged her with deep love and affection. The little girl began weeping with abundance of joy. Her mother began feeding her with her own hands. All the three ate together. The little girl didn't sleep that night; she kept talking to her parents, and her parents also stayed awake.

Just before the break of dawn another miracle took place. All the three were lying supine, gazing at the blue sky and twinkling stars, and talking to each other. And suddenly the twinkling stars began falling from the sky. Every star that fell and touched the earth, turned into a gold piece.

"My sweet little daughter! We shall have to leave as soon as the dawn breaks. So collect as many gold pieces as you can. Return to your village, buy a small home for yourself, and live happily. Yes, one more thing," said her mother fondling her with love, "We died even before we could have christened you. But now by God's grace it has become possible. From now on you will be known as Martha. Good-bye, my sweet little daughter! Good-bye!" saying this the parents of Martha began evanescing.

Martha raised her hand to say good-bye to her loving parents but they had disappeared by then. But she had a consolation that at least she would be able to see her parents once in a month and stay with them for one whole night.

Martha returned to her village, bought a small house for herself and lived happily ever after.

She could forget anything in the world, but she never forgot to go and meet her parents in the clearing of the forest once in a month on a particular night.

SEVEN KIDS AND A SLY WOLF

THERE was a small village nestled at the foot of the lower Himalayas; and at the outskirts of the village, from where the forest began, there was an abandoned hut which was very small. In this small hut, there lived a nanny goat with her seven kids. She was a widow as the billy goat had been gobbled up by a sly wolf living nearby.

It hadn't been a fine day a day before, as it had rained like billy-o throughout the day and night, and the nanny goat had not been able to go out to graze and bring food for her kids.

It was a fine morning today. She woke up, stretched her limbs in order to ward off her drowsiness and stood bolt upright. But there still was a drawn and haggard look about her eyes. She peeped out of the window to have a view of the sky, and was happy to see that there were no signs of clouds. The sky was absolutely clear. Sighing with relief she turned towards her kids and said, "Kids! I just looked outside to take a stock of the weather; the weather is fine and I shall be going out to graze and bring food for all of you. But what is not fine is that the cunning wolf, who killed and ate your father last month, is lurking outside. Be very careful, and don't open the door until I return," saying this she opened the door of the hut and instructing them to bolt the door firmly from inside, she left.

The wolf was hiding behind the bushes and waiting for the nanny goat to leave. He watched her until he lost sight of her. Then he stood on his fours and began moving towards the hut stealthily. He went quietly up to the door and knocked.

"Who is it?" asked one of the kids from inside.

"It's your mother, kids," said the wolf in a husky voice, "Open the door; I have brought food for all of you."

"Come on! stop kidding! You cannot be our mother," said all the seven kids in unison, "Our mother has a soft and sweet voice; not a husky voice like that of yours."

The wolf returned disappointed. He somehow managed to get some chalk and ate a lot of it to make his voice soft and sweet. He rehearsed again and again before going back to the hut—'Kids! Open the door; I am your mother.' And it was only after being fully satisfied with his voice, that he went to the hut again and knocked at the door.

"Kids! open the door; I am your mother," spoke the wolf in a soft and sweet voice as far as possible.

But the kids were smart. They peeped outside through a chink and saw a pair of black feet.

"No, no, you cannot be our mother! You managed to change your voice; but your feet are black; whereas my mother's feet are as white as snow. Stay away you cheat, you scoundrel! I know, you are the one who killed and ate our father; you are the one who widowed our mother and rendered us fatherless," said one of the kids.

Once again the cunning wolf returned disappointed. "What to do now?" he began thinking. Young and chubby kids were his favourite food. He wanted to get them and eat them at any cost. He knew there were seven kids inside. And getting a chance to eat them all at a time will leave him free from worries for food for days together.

Suddenly a bright idea flashed across his mind. He became very happy and set out to the painter's studio quickly. He knocked at the door of the studio and began waiting impatiently.

The painter was an elderly person. He was wearing horn-rimmed glasses. The door opened and the painter peeped out; he was shocked to see a big wolf standing before him, bearing his teeth in furious snarls, and lolling out his tongue. As if not able to believe his eyes, he held his glasses in one hand, rubbed them, huffed on them and settled them on his nose; and now what he saw was no different from what he had seen a moment ago.

"Hallo, dear wolf! What can I do for you?" said the painter. His voice trembled with theatrically controlled fear.

The cunning wolf was quick to understand that the painter was terribly scared. So, in order to take advantage of the situation, he spoke in a very heavy voice—

"Dear painter! Please paint my feet in white colour."

The painter couldn't understand why the wolf wanted his feet to be painted in white colour, but he couldn't dare ask him the reason.

He painted his feet in white and said goodbye to the wolf.

The wolf returned to the hut, rested his paws on the window sill; and this he did on purpose, so that the kids could see his white feet and let him in, and said in a soft tone—

"Kids! open the door; I am your mother. See what I have brought for you."

The kids saw a pair of white feet resting on the window sill, the voice too was soft and sweet, and this time they were totally outwitted by the cunning wolf. Soft and sweet voice and a pair of white feet was enough to give them to understand that their mother was asking them to open the door.

As soon as the door opened, the wolf pounced upon them. The kids realised the bitter truth, but alas, it was too late. There was no escaping. They began running around in a bid to save their lives. And in total confusion one kid slipped under the bed, the second one hid himself under the table and closed his eyes, thinking that by doing this he wouldn't be seen, the third one ran into the kitchen, the fourth one into the cupboard, the fifth one jumped into the wash-basin, the sixth one hid himself behind the oven, and the seventh one took refuge in the grandfather clock.

It was a horrendous scene. The kids were bleating; they were pleading for mercy, and the wolf was swallowing them one by one. He swallowed six kids one after the other. He did not care for the seventh one. Either he did not know counting, or he was too full.

Anyway...the seventh one, which had taken refuge in the grandfather clock, survived. The wolf had gone away.

The nanny goat returned in the evening, and was stunned to see the door of the hut open.

She hurried in. Everything in the room was out of place; some of the things lying upside down. The room was all topsy-turvy.

"Hey kids! Where are you?" she called out loud in a trembling voice. Tears welled up in her eyes. "Oh God! If only my kids had listened to my advice." Just as she was muttering these words, the seventh kid jumped out of the grandfather clock.

He began weeping bitterly to see his mother. Amid sobbing he narrated the whole story to her. Now she realised that the kids were not so much at fault.

She hugged him and consoled herself with the thought that at least one had survived. Suddenly an idea crept into her mind...

'The wolf may not have bolted my kids in gobbets; he may have swallowed them in a hurry, and if that be true, there is a faint chance of getting my kids back alive.'

This brought a ray of hope, and she began planning ways to tackle the situation.

"My dear sweet little kid! The wolf may not have gone too far. He has got six of my kids in his stomach; and this must have made it impossible for him to move. He must be lying somewhere near our hut. Let us go out and search for him. I go in this direction and you go in that; but be very careful," said the nanny goat.

Suddenly the kid saw the spoor of the wolf; he shouted excitedly, "Mother! Come, see the footprints of the wolf; he must have gone in this direction."

The nanny goat came running and saw the footprints of the wolf in the mud. The mother and the kid followed the wolf spoor and traced him lying supine under a banyan tree.

The wolf was snoring loudly. She ran to a garden nearby as fast as her legs could take her. There was a gardener working in it. She requested him to give her his pair of scissors.

"I can see movement in his stomach," said the nanny goat happily, "This means all your six brothers are still alive," saying this she began snipping at the skin of his stomach carefully.

All the kids came out one by one happily; though looking quite drowsy. She hugged and kissed each one of them with tears in her eyes.

"Kids! All of you go and bring as many pebbles as you can. Meanwhile, I shall go and bring a needle and thread from your tailor uncle. It won't take me much time."

The kids immediately began collecting pebbles and by the time she returned with needle and thread, they had collected more than the quantity required.

She filled up the stomach of the wolf with pebble and sutured it. They returned to their hut frolicking and gambolling.

It took a few days for the wolf to open his eyes; but he was feeling very uncomfortable. He was still lying on his back with his tongue lolled out, his eyes rolled back...feeling giddy.

It took the wolf another two days to gather enough strength to stand on his legs; he was feeling terribly thirsty. He used his last ounce of energy and began moving very slowly towards the nearby pond. Hearing the clattering sound of the pebbles coming from his stomach, he thought that it were the undigested bones of the kids which were clattering.

While returning after quenching his thirst, he saw the seven kids playing happily near the hut. They too saw him, but they didn't seem frightened; they were rather giggling at him. He was in a very strange state of predicament. He was feeling very hungry, yet his stomach was so full that he couldn't eat anything. The heaviness of his stomach had restricted his movement to such an extent that he could hardly move. Running and chasing his prey was simply out of question.

Suddenly he was jolted into wakefulness.

'How is it that these kids are playing here? I had eaten them up. How is it possible?'

Then he looked at his stomach which had ballooned beyond limits. Things got so inextricably mixed up that he had to console himself by telling—

'Come on! Don't be foolish! It cannot be the same kids. She may have given birth to another seven kinds.'

Everyday he would examine his inflated stomach, expecting it to deflate gradually; but it never did. Clattering sound from inside his stomach continued endlessly. His stomach continued to growl with hunger, but he was unable to eat anything.

And ultimately a day came when he died of starvation.

❏ ❏

THE SELFISH GIANT

ON the green heart of a smiling valley, which echoed with the calls of colourful birds and orioles, there was once a large mansion, called, "Fairy Dell" where lived a giant who was very selfish and cruel. He never allowed anyone to enter his mansion or garden.

He had planted a wide variety of fruit trees. Undoubtedly there were other gardens too, in that green and fertile valley, and though those gardens could boast of many a lovely blossom, nowhere could one come across the queen of all flowers—The Rose—in such beauty and variety. Some of the special quality of roses were christened 'Paul Neron', 'Black Prince', and 'Bride', etc.

Once the giant had to go out for seven days. When he returned, he saw a number of small children playing and running around in his garden. He became very angry and began chasing them. All the children scampered away, except one, who, out of nervousness, scrambled up a fruit tree. The selfish giant caught hold of him and thrashed him badly. The child went away weeping bitterly.

On the same day he erected a high wall around his garden. Now there was a big gate fixed to the wall that fenced his garden and entry of anyone was strictly prohibited.

Gradually, the spring came and the green valley became greener. In the gardens of others, the branches of fruit trees creaked with the weight of fruits, the flower plants were filled with innumerable number of flowers; but the selfish giant's garden yielded neither fruit nor flowers. It was still winter in his garden. He was surprised; but he failed to realise that trees and plants, apart from good soil, manure, and water, need love and affection also. it was impossible for him to understand that it was because of the innocent love of children that the trees and plants were yielding fruit and flowers.

The selfish giant would water the plants everyday, add more manure, but to no avail. He was surprised to see the trees and plants drying very fast.

"Coming and going of seasons is automatic. It has its own cycle; then why is it that my garden is deprived of spring season," thought the giant to himself. But he had no answer.

One morning, when he woke up, he heard some children giggling in his garden. He rushed out of his room, and what he saw was unbelievable. His fruit trees were laden with fruits, and flower plants filled with flowers of different colours. He also saw some small children still creeping in through a small hole in the wall.

"Oh! That's what makes the difference. These trees and plants missed the company of these children, and refused to yield anything," thought the giant to himself.

He came slowly to the garden wearing a broad smile on his face. But as soon as the children saw him, they began running away to save themselves from the wrath of the selfish giant. But the giant stopped them.

"No, no, dear children! Please don't run away. This garden is yours. You can play in this garden as long as you wish."

The children were simply astonished to hear what he said. He continued, "Dear children! I accept my mistake. I have been too cruel to you all." Then with tears in his eyes, he said, "Look, children! I am apologizing before you with folded hands. Please forgive me."

This made a positive effect on the children. They drew near him. The giant who was no more selfish, hugged and kissed them each. What more did the children want? They began playing with him, with his beard and long ears. The giant was enjoying it thoroughly. He gave them lots of fruit and nuts to eat.

Now the selfish giant had become their 'Giant Uncle'. Giant uncle said, "Children! From now onwards, this beautiful garden belongs not to me, but it belongs to every child in this world. You are free to come and play here. Bring as many friends as you like; eat as much fruit as you can....and if you don't come to play here, I shall beat you."

Hearing this the children began giggling and laughing.

Giant uncle took a pickaxe and began razing the wall that fenced his garden.

Giant uncle is no more, but that garden still exists where season is no bar. One can go and see that the garden is full of fruit and flowers in every season.

❑ ❑

THE GNOMES AND THE TAILOR

Once, a long long time ago, there was a tailor who was considered an expert in his job and was in great demand. But, as luck would have it, his customers began losing interest in him. They began calling his designs outdated. The tailor began having less and less orders; and a time came when he had no orders.

"I wonder what has happened to you. Your customers have lost their interest in you totally," said the tailor's wife irritably.

"What can I do? I am doing my best. Well! I think I should try on some new design of the jackets that I prepare. The problem with me now is that I have no money to invest. I have got only one piece of cloth left to make just one jacket," said the tailor scratching his baldhead.

He cut out the cloth in a new design in the evening, and thinking that he would sew the jacket together in the next morning, went to sleep. But next morning, when he sat down to work after finishing his breakfast, he noticed that the cut out cloth had already been sewn into a nice piece of jacket.

"How amazing!" said the tailor to his wife, "I am pleasantly surprised to see the quality of your work. I never knew that," saying this the tailor kissed his wife on her forehead.

"I don't understand a word you say. Tell me what makes you praise me so much," said the tailor's wife a little surprised.

"Why? Wasn't it you who sewed the jacket together in the night when I was asleep?" asked the tailor in disbelief.

"No, certainly not! What makes you think so?" I amn't half as good as you are in tailoring," said the wife.

"But then who else could have done it?" asked the surprised tailor.

They were talking thus when suddenly there was a knock on the door.

There was a customer who wanted to buy a jacket. He liked the jacket so much that he paid handsomely for it.

Encouraged by it he brought two pieces of cloth to prepare two jackets and saved a little for daily expenses. He again cut out the material in the night, only to be sewn in the next morning.

Next morning when he woke up, again there was a miracle. The cut out cloth had mysteriously transformed into two pieces of nicely stitched jackets.

Again there were two customers standing at his door. They looked at the jackets with admiration and paid heavily for it.

"We would like to have five more of such jackets. When do you think you could make it available to us?" said the customers.

The tailor looked at his wife. His wife said, "Sir! We shall work day and night and I think it will take us two days to make five jackets available to you."

The customers returned satisfied.

The tailor went to the market and brought five pieces of cloth for five jackets. Again the same thing happened.

The customers came two days later and willingly paid a very heavy price for the jackets. This went on for a long time; and the tailor was no more the same poor tailor. He had earned a lot and accumulated a lot of weath.

One night the tailor and his wife decided to unravel the mystery and see for themselves as to who are the ones who are being so kind to them. So instead of going to sleep in their beds, they hid themselves behind a curtain in a corner of their room.

It was hardly past midnight when they saw five little gnomes appearing suddenly from nowhere. First they danced for a while holding each other's hands and then they sat down to stitch the jackets together from the cut out material.

The tailor and his wife found it hard to believe their eyes. The tailor had cut out cloth for ten jackets in the night, and the gnomes took hardly any time to sew them together; and that too with such precision and perfection.

The gnomes, after having finished their work, began dancing and singing—

'Go and tell the tailor,
I am very-very happy,
God has blessed me with a son,
tell him to sew me a nappy.
I am very-very happy...'

The tailor's wife was so moved to hear them sing thus that she immediately decided to sew a nappy for their child and some nice sets of clothes for them too.

They sang and danced and disappeared.

It took the tailor and his wife the whole day to sew a few nappies for the baby gnome, and some waistcoats, jackets, trousers, socks, and shirts for the gnomes.

It was again past midnight when the tailor and his wife saw the five gnomes appearing from nowhere.

They began dancing holding each other's hands; and after they had finished dancing, they began searching for cut out cloth for sewing, but instead, they saw a few nappies and a few beautiful looking nicely stitched set of clothes. They immediately knew it was for them. They quickly put on the clothes and began posing before a mirror from different angles.

"I knew that the tailor and his wife are very nice and kind-hearted. See what nice nappies they have swen for our baby gnome," said one gnome.

"Yes! I agree! Our clothes are also very beautiful. Now we can throw away our rags," said the other one.

"I wish we could make friends with them," said the third one.

"Yes! But only if they could keep a secret of it," said the fourth one.

And before the fifth one could say anything, the tailor and his wife came out from behind the curtain.

The gnomes began fidgeting nervously.

The tailor's wife said, "Please don't get nervous. We have done all this to express our gratitude; but this is nothing as compared to what you have done for us. We are indeed indebted to you all."

The oldest gnome stepped forward and said, "You two are very nice and kind-hearted. And we like such people. I saw your honesty and poverty and we decided to make your life easy."

"Thank you very much for everything. It is this kind act of yours that has made me wealthy. I don't know how to repay," said the tailor.

"Oh don't worry about that. Just be kind to others, and that's enough," said the fifth gnome who had all along been silent.

"There is a request," said the tailor's wife, " Could we see the baby gnome?"

"Oh yes! Why not? We shall bring him tomorrow along with his mother," said the baby gnome's father.

And next night the tailor and his wife didn't have to hide behind curtains. They were sitting and waiting for their little guests. The little guests appeared at the right hour. They were seven; because they had included the baby gnome and his mother also in the team.

The tailor's wife took the chubby looking baby gnome in her lap and was overwhelmed to see the baby gnome giving a cute smile.

This time the tailor and his wife also danced with the gnomes holding each other's hands. And while they were about to leave, they gave nice gifts and some very nice set of clothes to baby gnome's mother also.

"Don't be afraid! Come and see us whenever you feel like. You can trust us; we promise to keep a secret of it," said the tailor's wife.

The gnomes parted singing—
'Call us at the time of need,
we shall come here indeed.'

❑ ❑